IN ANGER

Uthman Hutchinson

illustrated by
Abdulmuttalib Fahema

First Edition
(1416 AH / 1995 AC)

In Anger and Other Stories
ISBN : 0-915957-46-9

Library of Congress Catalogue Card Number : 95-080048

Published by **amana publications**
10710 Tucker Street, Suite B
Beltsville, Maryland 20705-2223 USA
Tel: (301) 595-5777   Fax: (301) 595-5888

Printed in the United States of America by International Graphics
10710 Tucker Street, Beltsville, Maryland 20705-2223 USA
Tel: (301) 595-5999   Fax: (301) 595-5888

Contents

IN ANGER

Muhammad's heart was pounding like crazy. Sweat was dripping off him and his breath was rasping through his chest. He circled with the other boy, watching for any move that might signal another attack.

The other boy feigned to the right and stepped in with a left-right combination to the head. Muhammad dodged and blocked and counter punched. The punch was too slow and Muhammad found himself trying to block a kick to the chest, and then another. Then, suddenly, he was on the ground. He rolled away and was up, furious now. He began to attack, punch after punch at the other boy. He was fighting wildly now, and he knew it, but he couldn't stop himself. Muhammad was backing the other boy up against the wall.

"Stop!"

Muhammad heard the order, but he was so angry he didn't obey.

"Stop!"

Still Muhammad kept on, and then he was spun around and suddenly lying on his back. The wind was completely knocked out of him and he was clutching his stomach, working his mouth, unable to breathe. He pulled in a half breath and then another and then the air was rasping in and out again. All of the fight and the anger was knocked out of him.

"I told you to stop," a quiet voice said. There was a hand on his shoulder and Brother Yusuf was kneeling over him, looking into his eyes. "Are you all right?"

Muhammad nodded.

"Okay, get up off the mat and bow to your opponent."

Muhammad stood and straightened the top of his white karate 'gi' where it had fallen open. He pulled his orange belt back down over his hips and around so the knot was in front. Then the two boys moved to the center of the mat and bowed to each other as a sign of respect to end the match.

Brother Yusuf chose two more students to spar before the end of the class, but Muhammad couldn't even pay attention to the match. He felt ashamed and angry at himself. Not only had he lost the match, he had completely lost his temper and acted like a fool!

When the match was over, all the boys lined up to go into the locker room to change.

"Muhammad," said Brother Yusuf. "I want to see you for a second."

Muhammad came and sat down in front of his teacher who was now sitting cross legged on the mat.

"'Stop' means stop," said Brother Yusuf. "You have to learn to control yourself." He watched Muhammad for any reaction, but Muhammad was staring down at the mat. Brother Yusuf decided to be hard on him.

"Real life isn't TV," he said. "You don't get in a fight and get mad and then destroy someone. Those are just lies. If you get in a real fight and get mad, they destroy you. When you lose control, you're finished; and that counts for everything, not just fighting. What do you think we do all those exercises for? If you don't learn self control in this class, I don't even want to see you; you're out!"

Muhammad still sat there with his head down and his eyes on the mat.

"Have you got a book at home of the sayings of the Prophet, peace be upon him?" Brother Yusuf asked. "Have you got a hadith* collection?"

"Yes," said Muhammad, speaking for the first time.

"Okay, next class is Tuesday. By then I want you to find a hadith about controlling anger and memorize it in Arabic and English. Then I want you to practice it when you get angry. It does you absolutely no good to learn it if you're not going to do what it says. Remember, whether you stay in this class or not depends on you controlling your temper. Now go on," he said. "Go get changed."

When Muhammad entered the locker room, everybody was already gone except for Daud and Brian, who were sitting on a bench, talking. All three were getting picked up and taken

---

* Words or actions of the Prophet Muhammad, peace be upon him, which were recorded.

home by Brian's mother.

"Did you get kicked out?" asked Daud.

"No," said Muhammad.

"You're lucky," said Daud. "I've only seen him give someone a 'love tap' once before to stop a match, and that guy got kicked out on the spot."

"He didn't say it exactly, but I got the impression that this is my last chance," said Muhammad. He picked up his street clothes from where they sat on the bench, and went around behind the row of lockers to dress in private. None of the boys had lockers here. They only used this school two evenings a week to hold karate class.

"You really lost your temper at the end of the match there," said Brian. "You should have seen Brother Yusuf's face when you didn't stop on the second command. I never saw him move so fast."

"You've got to learn to control your temper," said Daud.

"I know," Muhammad called over the lockers, and he did know, but it wasn't so simple. "It's easy for you to say that, you've had three years to learn to control yours. I haven't even been at it a year yet." Even Muhammad himself knew that was a pretty lame excuse.

"It shouldn't take that long," said Daud. "Look at Brian. He started later than you did, and he doesn't have a problem."

"Yeah, I don't have a problem," echoed Brian, winking

at Daud.

"What's all this talk all of a sudden about me having a problem?" thought Muhammad. "Well, you're not sparring a lot yet," he said to Brian. "Just wait till you begin sparring, and see how easy it is."

"When I start sparring I don't intend to get mad at all. I intend to make my opponent mad," said Brian.

Daud laughed. "That's the idea," he said.

Muhammad came around the end of the lockers, buckling up his belt.

"Seriously," said Daud. "What did Brother Yusuf say?"

"He told me to memorize a hadith about anger in Arabic and English for next class and put it into practice."

"What's all this stuff about 'hadith' you guys are always talking about?" asked Brian. "Hadith is something your Prophet said, right?"

"Right," said Muhammad.

"So, how is memorizing that going to help you keep your temper?"

"It's all basic, practical stuff," said Muhammad.

"Human nature doesn't change," said Daud, "and the Prophet, peace be upon him, knew human nature inside out."

"A lot of it's instructions on how to deal with different situations," added Muhammad. "It's like a guide book; you know, when this thing happens, do this, when that thing happens, do that. When you follow it, it really works."

"I'd like to see that," said Brian, skeptically.

"Oh, you'll see," said Muhammad.

"Brother Yusuf's going to test you on this. You know that don't you?" warned Daud.

"I'll be ready for him," said Muhammad, but inside he wasn't quite so confident. He'd have to find the right hadith and really make it work.

When he arrived home, Muhammad went straight to the book shelf in the living room. He took out the first volume of the "Sahih Al-Bukhari" collection of hadith and opened up the index. What he was looking for could have been in a few different places. He took out three separate volumes and started reading. After an hour he'd found one hadith about anger in "Sahih Al-Bukhari" and two more in a different collection of hadith.

"I'll memorize all three of them," thought Muhammad.

The second two hadith were, "Anger comes from the Devil, the Devil was created of fire, and fire is extinguished only with water; so when one of you becomes angry he should perform wudu*." and "When one of you becomes angry while standing he should sit down. If the anger leaves him, well and good; otherwise he should lie down." Muhammad felt these

---

* Washing face, forearms and feet, done before the prayer.

were both very practical advice and easy to use, except for one thing. In a sparring match you couldn't suddenly stop and go make wudu or sit down. For ordinary circumstances though, they were just perfect.

The first hadith was, "The strong man is not one who wrestles well but the strong man is one who controls himself when he is angry." This one seemed to be tailored to the conditions of a match, but it didn't involve an action to take, but rather something to keep in mind. Together, he felt the three hadith were a perfect combination.

"Dinner, Muhammad," said Muhammad's sister, Fatima, who was standing beside the couch. He hadn't noticed her come in.

"Okay," he said. He put aside the two books he needed and returned the other volumes to the book shelf.

"What are you copying?" asked Fatima.

"Just some hadith," answered Muhammad.

"Come on," called Mr. Saeed. "We'll miss the prayer at the mosque if we don't eat now."

When the whole family was seated at the table, Mr. Saeed said, "Bismillah," In the name of Allah, and they all began passing around the food.

"How was karate class tonight?" asked Mr. Saeed.

"Fine," said Muhammad.

"I want to take karate too," said Jamaal

"You'll have to wait till you're a little older," said Mrs. Saeed.

Jamaal already had his hands up in front of his face though. They were open straight, rigid, and he was moving them in tiny circles. In his mind he was a deadly karate master. "Ayeeeee-a!" he squealed and chopped at an imaginary foe.

"Mommy!" complained Fatima, whose milk he had almost spilled.

"Jamaal!" said Mr. Saeed with a warning tone.

"Not at the table," said Mrs. Saeed.

Jamaal picked up his fork, and popping a piece of meat into his mouth, chewed happily. He had just single handedly taken out the biggest evil warlord in the county.

"What hadith were you copying out?" asked Mrs. Saeed, deciding to change the subject.

"It's just an assignment for Brother Yusuf for the next karate class," Muhammad replied.

"That's interesting," said Mr. Saeed. "He has you studying hadith along with karate?"

"Well, it's just something special for me," Muhammad admitted.

"Oh?" said Mr. Saeed.

"Mommy," said Fatima. "Did the Prophet, peace be upon him, know karate?"

"No," answered Mrs. Saeed. "Karate came later from

Japan."

"He knew wrestling!" said Jamaal.

"Yes," agreed Mrs. Saeed. "He knew wrestling, and he knew how to fight."

"He was a great wrestler!" said Jamaal, smiling smugly at his sister.

"So, what hadith did Brother Yusuf have you looking up?" asked Mr. Saeed.

"I'm supposed to find something the Prophet, peace be upon him, said about controlling anger and memorize it in both Arabic and English."

"Ah," said Mr Saeed, who understood the implications immediately. He knew that Muhammad had been sparring a lot in class lately. "It's not so easy to do," he said, "especially in a fight."

"What's not so easy to do?" asked Jamaal, who had been paying more attention to his potatoes than to the conversation.

"Control your anger," said Fatima, letting Jamaal know by her tone of voice that she was old enough to follow the whole conversation *and* eat potatoes.

"Oh," said Jamaal, unfazed. "The Prophet was great at that too!"

The weekend passed quickly and Tuesday evening came. As he stood in the locker room dressing, Muhammad went over the three hadith he had learned to make sure he knew them correctly in both languages. When he was ready, he went into the gym and approached Brother Yusuf as the other boys were coming in.

"Peace be upon you," said Brother Yusuf.

"And upon you be peace," said Muhammad. "I've come to tell you the hadith I memorized." He went on to tell Brother Yusuf both sayings in both languages and his reasons for picking them.

"Good," said Brother Yusuf. "Now keep them with you and use them when you have to."

"He talks about them as if they were weapons," thought Muhammad.

The first part of class was warm-up exercises and drills, as always, and the last part was sparring. It was getting near the end of the class, but Muhammad was not called up to spar although all of the other orange and yellow belts had been. "Maybe he's just going to let me stew in my own juices, and not call me at all," thought Muhammad.

Just ten minutes before the end of class, Brother Yusuf called his name.

Muhammad went up and stood in the middle of the mat, waiting. Brother Yusuf took a moment and surveyed the whole class, as if deciding who to match against Muhammad. Then his eyes stopped on one boy. "Daud," he said.

That was a shock for Muhammad. He had never faced

anyone so advanced except for Brother Yusuf himself. Daud was a brown belt! Muhammad was afraid he knew what might be coming. "No," he thought, "Daud's my best friend, he'll go easy on me."

Daud might have gone easy on him, but what Muhammad didn't know was that Brother Yusuf had taken Daud aside and spoken to him before class.

"I'm going to put you in to spar with Muhammad today," he had said. "I know you're best friends, and that's part of the reason I want you to do it. I want you to press him and I want you to press him hard. Don't hurt him, but I want you to confuse him and hurt his pride. I want you to make him mad."

Daud looked surprised.

"If you want him to learn karate, and a lot more besides, you'll do it," said Brother Yusuf. "If I didn't think he could pass this test, I wouldn't give it to him. He would have already been out of my class."

Daud hoped Brother Yusuf was right, and he hoped the next ten minutes of sparring wouldn't ruin his best friendship forever.

As soon as the match opened Daud put both fists in Muhammad's face in quick succession and then delivered a side kick to his friend's stomach. The punches were stopped expertly at the right places so that the thick padding of the gloves barely pushed against Muhammad's face. The kick was delivered a little harder. The fighters' feet were also padded and Muhammad managed to get his arm down to block the force of the kick. Daud danced away to the other side of the mat. He put on his best competition match form. It was a mixture of extreme cockiness and speed with a lot of shouting when he struck. All of this was designed to intimidate an opponent.

The next few minutes could best be described as a terrible beating delivered softly. The full force of the blows never touched Muhammad's body, but they did touch his pride.

At first Muhammad couldn't believe it. He was by turns, shocked, angry and then afraid. Afraid of Daud! He clung to the knowledge that this was only a test and to the hadith he had learned, like a drowning man clings to a log. "The strong man controls his anger, the strong man controls his anger," he told himself again and again. "Control my anger?" he thought, "I can't even control my body!"

He finally lost his temper when his legs were swept out from under him for the third time. Each time he stood, they were swept out again and he landed hard, and there was nothing he could do about it. Then Daud was dancing all around him, taunting him to get up. Muhammad lay there engulfed in fury. "The strong man controls his anger," he thought desperately over and over. He could storm off the mat and never come back, why should he take this? He could tackle Daud and kill him wrestling! "The strong man controls his anger!"

Then Muhammad was slowly dragging himself up from the mat. He had a precarious hold on himself again. He wasn't going to quit and he wasn't going to let Daud defeat him. Daud could beat his body all he wanted, but he wouldn't make him fail this test! Oh, for the joy of just getting one glove on him, though! It seemed to be Muhammad's only wish.

Muhammad moved toward Daud now. His arms were like lead, he could hardly keep them up. He moved up almost to striking distance and then let both his arms drop with a groan. Daud struck instantaneously, putting his left hand up against Muhammad's head and following it with a right. Muhammad let the left go, without any chance of stopping it, but judged correctly that the right would follow and managed to get his right glove up to deflect it. Then, at the same instant he counter-punched over Daud's right shoulder with his left hand. He put his last remaining strength into the maneuver and connected hard against Daud's headgear. Daud lost his balance for an instant and stepped back, eying Muhammad with sudden respect. If it hadn't been for the padding on his head and the thick gloves, he could have been knocked out by that punch!

"Pull your punches!" ordered Brother Yusuf.

Muhammad just managed a slight smile of triumph before Daud renewed his attack.

The last minute of the match was just a blur for Muhammad until Brother Yusuf finally called time. Then he and

Daud bowed to each other and joined the rest of the students kneeling on the mat.

Muhammad was a mess. He was drenched with sweat and he ached all over. He felt like he would never get his breath back. He had passed the test! He'd taken the worst Daud could do and had held his temper! Why had Daud been so hard on him, though? He didn't need to kill him! "You'd think he wanted me to fail," thought Muhammad bitterly. "He's supposed to be my friend!" The more he thought about it, the madder he grew.

Brother Yusuf was pleased. He watched the students file into the locker room with a stern face. Only when the last student was gone, did he smile. Alhamdulillah!"* he exclaimed. He paced up the mat with his hands on his hips and paced back down. He couldn't keep from smiling. It was great when a student learned a new move or technique, but there was no more intense pleasure than when a student really understood a principle. Brother Yusuf shook his head. He doubted if Muhammad would ever forget the lesson he'd learned today.

Muhammad had entered the locker room with his anger still rising. There were Daud and the others smiling. Daud was putting out his hand, but Muhammad didn't want to shake it. Why should he shake his hand? Muhammad's face was set into

---

* All praise is for Allah.

a hard mask of control as he passed straight by Daud. With the anger inside him he didn't trust himself to open his mouth or even meet anyone's eyes. He walked around the edge of the lockers and up and down between the rows. The other boys could hear him still gasping from the fight. Then he walked off by the showers. After a couple of minutes they couldn't hear him any more. Brian went over to see what he was up to and came back.

"What's he doing?" asked Daud.

"He was washing his face and forearms and feet like you do before you pray, and then he lay down on a bench. I tried to talk to him, but he just waived me away."

Daud smiled. "He's doing what the hadith says, to get rid of anger," he said.

"Man, I thought he was going to explode when he first came in here," said Brian.

The two boys dressed while Muhammad lay on the bench. The others had already dressed and gone. Muhammad got up and went into the shower to make wudu again.

"Muhammad!" shouted Daud. "Are you mad at me, or what?"

The boys waited for an answer but none came. Then Muhammad appeared around the end of the lockers. "Hey," he said with a grin. "You're the one who should be mad at me. I got you with one beautiful punch on the side of the head!"

Muhammad and Daud slapped their hands together.

"Yeah, you did that," said Daud.

After a few minutes the three boys sat outside on a bicycle rack, waiting for Daud's father to come pick them up.

"That hadith stuff really seems to work," said Brian.

"Every time," said Muhammad.

"Well, maybe you could look up something for me," suggested Brian.

"Sure," said Muhammad. "What do you need?"

"How about something to keep me awake in geometry class?"

Daud burst out laughing.

"Sure," said Muhammad. "It might take us a while, but I'm sure we can find something."

FAJR TROUBLE

"I just can't seem to do it," complained Mustafa.

"Come on, it's not very difficult," said Muhammad.

"That's easy for you to say, you've got someone to wake you up. I've always been a heavy sleeper. Now that my mom went away to stay with grandma till she gets better, I'm the only one home at dawn. My dad doesn't arrive home from work till almost seven o'clock."

"So, use an alarm clock," said Muhammad.

"That's what I did this morning and I just turned it off without waking up. I don't even remember a thing. I slept right through the dawn prayer."

"Use two clocks," suggested Muhammad.

Mustafa just shrugged.

"How does your mother usually wake you up?"

"She shakes me and literally drags me out of bed. Sometimes she even walks me down the hall and puts water on my face. I'm like a bear in hibernation when I sleep. It's almost impossible for me to wake up."

Muhammad laughed for a moment and then the two boys sat in silence on the bench outside the school. Recess was almost finished.

"I hate missing the fajr* prayer and having to make it up after the sun rises," said Mustafa. "It seems to throw my whole day off."

"I know what you mean," said Muhammad.

"When my dad comes home and finds me sleeping he looks at me like I'm just a little kid again who can't take care of himself. Everything gets late and I end up only finishing half my breakfast before I run out the door for the bus without my coat on. It's been two days like that now."

Most of the children were starting to go back inside the school now.

"Try putting two clocks across the room from you," said Muhammad. "That way you'll have to get out of bed to turn them off."

"Okay," said Mustafa as the two boys stood up. "It's worth giving a try."

The next morning at five thirty everything was quiet at Mustafa's house. The house was a little cold, with the heat turned down, but in Mustafa's bed it was perfectly warm. Mustafa was riding his bicycle down a long, sweeping hill on a warm, sunny day. His bike was big and although he was pedaling it, it was somehow motorized. He was traveling very fast. Suddenly the two alarms went off in Mustafa's room. In his

---

* A dawn prayer in congregation; one of five prayers a day for Muslims.

dream, Mustafa turned and looked over his shoulder at the road behind him. A whole pack of professional cyclists was coming up fast. They were ringing the bells on their handlebars for him to pull aside and let them pass. They were right on his rear tire now, their ringing grew louder and more insistent. Mustafa was roused to action. He dragged himself slowly up out of his dream, but not wholly into wakefulness. Then, oddly, things grew quiet again and Mustafa drifted back into a dreamless slumber.

"Mustafa... Mustafa!" The voice was loud and insistent. "Come on and get yourself up from there!"

Mustafa's father was standing in the doorway with his hands on his hips. As Mustafa lifted his head and squinted open his eyes, he saw his father shake his head in rebuke and turn to walk back down the hall. "You'd better make up your prayer and get going or you'll be late for school," he called back. "Your eggs are almost done cooking."

For a moment Mustafa was completely disoriented. He was staring at the leg of a chair where it met the carpet. He propped himself up on one elbow. Two alarm clocks lay at odd angles beneath the chair where he had placed them the night before. Both alarms were turned off. Mustafa himself was sprawled across the floor between his bed and the chair, with one arm still clutching the blankets he had pulled down from the bed to keep himself warm. Mustafa groaned. He didn't remember a thing. He couldn't even remember his bicycle

dream.

"That's a good one," Muhammad laughed.

"It's hopeless," said Mustafa.

"Why don't you put the alarms under your pillow?" suggested Daud.

All three boys were eating lunch together beside the basketball court. Daud had joined in their deliberations.

"I tried putting a clock under the pillow before," said Mustafa. "It didn't work. I just turned off the alarm."

"It works for me," said Daud. "It wakes me right up."

Suddenly Muhammad had an idea. "Get your father to telephone you," he said. "Do you have a phone jack in your room?"

"Sure," said Mustafa. "That's a great idea!"

"It's so simple," said Muhammad. "He can keep talking to you so you don't go back to sleep."

"He can talk you right out of bed and out into the hall," said Daud. "There's no way you'll get back to sleep then."

"Fantastic!" said Mustafa. "Gentlemen, I think we may have something here! We may just de-hibernate the bear yet."

That evening Mustafa arranged for his father to call him the next morning at five thirty, sharp. Before he went to bed he moved the telephone from his parent's room into his. He plugged the cord into the wall jack and placed the telephone on the side table by his bed. He even switched the volume up to maximum on the bottom of the phone. That was bound to work!

The phone rang seven times before Mustafa even picked it up. "Hello," he drawled.

"Mustafa, this is your father," said a voice at the other end of the line.

"Father's not here," mumbled Mustafa, and he put the phone back on the receiver.

This time the phone only rang three times before Mustafa picked it up.

"Yeah."

"Mustafa, this is your father! Do not hang up. Mustafa, do not hang up! This is your father speaking to you!"

In his half-sleep, Mustafa's brow wrinkled in bewilderment.

"This is your father, telling you to get up out of bed! Stand up now!"

"Okay, dad." Mustafa fought the covers ineptly with his free hand and then settled back down with a half snore.

"MUSTAFA, GET UP!" shouted his father.

Mustafa threw back the covers and jumped out of bed. He stood there with the phone to his ear, his eyes closed.

"Mustafa, listen to me," said the voice over the phone. "Pick up the phone unit."

Mustafa fumbled across the table with his free hand and picked it up.

"It's time for fajr," said the voice. "Go out into the hall."

Mustafa began to shuffle.

"Don't put down the phone," the voice said.

Mustafa had reached the doorway.

"Don't put down the phone, Mustafa. Do you hear me?"

"Yeah."

"Now, go down the hallway to the bathroom and make wudu."

Mustafa shuffled down the hall.

"Now, Mustafa, listen to me. Turn on the li... "

Mustafa shuffled a little further down the hall. As he passed the light switch, the phone line became taut, and POP, the plug pulled out from the wall in his room. The phone went dead.

Mustafa stood still, teetering where he was. "Not home," he mumbled. The hand with the receiver dropped to his side and the telephone itself dropped to the floor. Mustafa turned back to his room, still holding the receiver and dragging the phone behind him. He bumped into a door frame and awkwardly turned into his parent's room. When his shins hit the edge of the bed he climbed up over it, pulled back the covers, and snuggled down inside. He curled his hands up under the pillow, still holding the receiver in his hand, and slept like a baby.

Mustafa just sat there, frowning, staring at the ground. All the other boys around him were laughing.

"It's serious!" complained Mustafa.

"I'm sorry," said Muhammad, trying to sober himself up.

"Man!" said Lateef.

Daud sat on the bench, still shaking with silent laughter, and William had to turn away to compose himself.

"Get a pet rooster," suggested Lateef.

"Set off the fire alarm," suggested Daud. "That'll wake you up."

"Very funny," said Mustafa, still frowning with his elbows on his knees and his face in his hands.

"Water!" said Muhammad. "Water will wake you up."

"Sure," said William. "Put a bowl of water by your bed."

"I'm liable to spill it all over," said Mustafa.

"Then you have to get into the bathroom somehow," said Muhammad.

"I know," said Daud. "Make a trail of alarm clocks leading to the bathroom!"

"Yeah," said Lateef.

"Yeah!"

"I only have two alarm clocks," said Mustafa. He was not enthusiastic.

"How about a clock radio?" asked William. "Do you have a clock radio?"

"Yeah," said Mustafa, sitting up for the first time. "That might work."

"Sure," said Muhammad. "Make a trail into the bathroom; one clock in your bedroom, one down the hall, and the clock radio in the bathroom. Once you get in there you just put some water on your face and you're set."

"Battle plan three," said Mustafa wearily. "Ready, set, action."

Mustafa had it all set up. One alarm clock was right in his doorway on the floor. The second clock was halfway down the hall. The clock radio was in the bathroom, sitting on the toilet tank with the volume all the way up. Everything was set to go off at exactly the same time.

It wasn't a dream that could admit bells into it, or maybe the ringing noise was just too loud. In any case, Mustafa's dream was suddenly gone and all that was left was the clamor of alarm clocks and buzzers in the cold darkness. Mustafa stood up out of bed and grabbed his blankets around his shoulders. He made for the door and kicked the clock before he found it on his hands and knees and smacked it hard, hitting the off button. Oddly, the ringing didn't stop. Mustafa continued down the hallway on all fours. He found the second clock and smacked that one off too. Again, the noise did not stop.

Mustafa groped his way up against the wall into a standing position and continued back toward the blaring sound. There was a tremendous buzzing noise with shouted advertisements coming from the bathroom. Mustafa fumbled his hands across the sink and clutched the clock radio. He fumbled with the buttons and the buzzer went off. The channel changed. Then the buzzer went back on. Suddenly the radio was screaming out high frequency noise louder than ever.

Mustafa groaned in exasperation and reeled to his left. The plug popped out of the socket and Mustafa exhaled a pure sigh of relief into the sudden silence. He sat down on the edge of the tub. All was darkness and calm around him. Mustafa pulled his blankets a little tighter over his shoulder and sighed again. The silence was wonderful.

Later that morning when Mustafa's father found him, Mustafa was curled up inside the bathtub. His blankets were pulled tightly around him and the clock radio was cradled to his chest as if it were a new born baby.

"Unbelievable," said Muhammad.

He and Mustafa were seated at a table in the small school library. Mustafa sat shaking his head with a sheepish grin. "It's unbelievable to me too," he said.

The two boys were sitting inside because recess outside had become just impossible. By now the whole school knew about Mustafa's problem. The latest episode had gotten around as a tremendous joke. Mustafa hadn't been able to eat his lunch in peace. He and Muhammad had given up and come inside.

"Man, I'll never live this down," said Mustafa.

"You know, said Muhammad. "I think we've been going

about solving this the wrong way."

"How do you mean?" asked Mustafa.

"Well, we've been looking at our own solutions when there might already be a solution from the Prophet, peace be upon him. I mean, let's look at what he said about getting up for the Fajr prayer. Maybe there will be something there to help."

"Yeah," said Mustafa as he looked around the book shelves in the library. "I'll look in the "Sahih Muslim" collection of hadith, and you look in 'Sahih Al-Bukhari'."

"Sure," said Muhammad, "I know your game, you take the collection with only four volumes while I get nine volumes to carry."

Muhammad laughed. "Look, I'll get out "Mishkat-ul-Masabih" too," he said. "That way I'll have more to carry than you will. Will that make you happy?"

The two boys got up and went to the shelves and soon they came back with their arms loaded and began to look through the books' indexes.

"Boy," said Muhammad, as he ran his finger down past the hundreds of entries. "It's amazing how those first Muslims memorized everything the Prophet Muhammad said and did."

"Yeah," agreed Mustafa, "and then compiled it all and saved it!"

The boys leafed through the different volumes. "Here we go," said Muhammad. "This looks like it might be something."

"What have you got there?" asked Mustafa.

"It's volume two of the Mishkat," said Muhammad. "'The Merits Of Prayer.' Listen to this. 'Umara bin Ruwaiba reported: I heard Allah's* Messenger (peace and blessings of Allah be upon him) as saying: None who would observe the prayer before the rising of the sun and the setting of the sun, the dawn and the afternoon prayers, would get into Hellfire.'"

"Let me see," said Mustafa. He reread the hadith and continued reading down the page. "Listen to this," he said. "'He who observes two cool prayers, he would get into Paradise.' That means the Fajr prayer and the afternoon prayer."

"Or it could mean the fajr prayer and the night prayer," said Muhammad.

"That's right," agreed Mustafa. He continued reading. Every once in a while he made a sound of approval as he read. "This is full of things about Fajr," he said. Then Mustafa read something which made him stop altogether. He read it again.

Muhammad, who was watching his friend, saw his face change. "What is it?" he asked.

Mustafa shook his head to himself as he closed the book. His face was grim. "Nothing," he mumbled. He looked at his watch. "It's time for class," he said. "Let's get these books back on the shelf."

---

* God's.

Muhammad purposefully took a long time getting his books on the shelf and then fixing their order. Mustafa was done and waiting at the table, looking out the window, thinking. He roused himself from his thoughts and looked at his watch again. "Are you coming?" he asked.

"You go ahead," said Muhammad.

When Mustafa left, Muhammad found the book Mustafa had been reading. He would be late for class, but he wanted to see what had hit Mustafa so hard. He found the right chapter and began to scan the hadith. There it was, Muhammad was sure of it. It was only a short hadith.

"No prayer is more burdensome to the hypocrites than the dawn and night prayers, and if they were to know what (immeasurable reward) lies in them they would come even if they had to crawl."

It was the fear of hypocrisy that had struck Mustafa. Muhammad wondered if it would be enough to make him wake up in the mornings.

That night Mustafa sat thinking and making dua* before going to bed. He thought he knew why he couldn't get up for the fajr prayer. It was simply a lack of motivation, lack of intention. Now he was scared though. He did not want to be one of those who said with their tongues what they did not do with their

---

* A private prayer, asking for something.

hands. He did not want to be a proven liar.

Before he turned out the light he checked the alarm clock and set it on the table by his bed. He switched off the light and lay back on his pillow. God willing, I will wake up tomorrow, he told himself. I will wake up.

That was the last thing Mustafa remembered until he was suddenly awake in the dark. He was wide awake, and he knew it was Fajr time. He grabbed the alarm clock and peered at it's luminous face. It was set to go off at any moment. Mustafa pushed the button down and swung his feet out onto the floor. Later that morning at school, when Muhammad pulled up on the bus, he could see that Mustafa was surrounded by the other boys of the fifth grade. As Muhammad stepped off the bus, Mustafa looked over and flashed him a thumbs up sign. Muhammad returned the sign with a big smile.

Three days later Mustafa's mother returned. Over dinner that night she asked Mustafa if he had had any trouble while she was gone. "No," he said simply, "no trouble at all."

WHAT'S IN A NAME

"Hey, Mo!"

"Don't call me Mo!" It was the third time Muhammad had told him! "My name is Muhammad."

"Okay, so, you ready, Mo?"

Muhammad just kept his temper and squatted, waiting for the count. He turned his attention from the boy who had been speaking, to the larger boy directly in front of him. It was Muhammad's job to get past that boy as soon as the ball was hiked back to the quarterback. The quarterback was the other boy who had been teasing Muhammad to get him rattled.

"Twenty-four, sixteen, thirty-two, hike!"

The ball snapped back and Muhammad was charging up against the boy in front of him. They clashed hard, the boy fending Muhammad off with his forearms and elbows. Muhammad drove him back a few yards and then tried to go around him. The boy stuck with Muhammad, guarding the quarterback. Muhammad spun to the side to try to go around the boy again, but by this time the ball had already been thrown. It was a long, spiraling pass past the goal line. The receiver was there and he grabbed the ball, clutching it to his chest.

"Touchdown!"

"All right!"

"All right, Casey!"

The receiver who had caught the ball was circling back toward the quarterback, high stepping, with both arms raised in the air and the football in one hand. When he reached the quarterback they both slapped hands high in the air. "Casey!" said the receiver. The four boys who made up the football team were all congratulating each other.

Muhammad's team was not in quite the same mood. The score was thirty-six to nothing. Muhammad was also annoyed for other reasons. The quarterback, whose name was Qasim, had been teasing Muhammad ever since Muhammad had asked him why he didn't use his real name.

"That's enough for me," said Daud. "I've got to be home by four."

"Yeah," agreed Brian, "I've had enough."

"Me too," said Doug.

The game began to break up, with boys in twos and threes wandering off toward their homes.

"You've got to admit, he's a great quarterback," said Daud.

"Yeah," agreed Muhammad, "but I don't have to like him."

Qasim was new in the neighborhood. His parents were from Jordan, but he had been brought up in America. Neither he nor his parents ever came to the mosque, though they had moved in almost a month ago. They didn't seem to have anything to do with the other Muslims in the area. It was Daud who had organized the football game with some of the new kids. They were going to have a game every Saturday.

"Hey, wait up you guys!" Qasim was running to catch up to the three boys. "Man, did you see that long bomb I threw? Beautiful, huh?"

"Yeah," agreed Brian. "You've got a good arm, all right."

"What do you think, Mo?"

"I think you should stop calling me Mo, Casey," said Muhammad sarcastically.

"Hey, Casey's my name, don't wear it out," said Qasim jauntily.

"It's not your name," said Daud. "Your name's Qasim, and it has a meaning to it. Are you ashamed to use it or something? Do you even know what it means?"

"All that's got nothing to do with me," answered Qasim, for the first time sounding defensive. "Anyway, Casey's easer for people to say."

"What? Do you think Americans are too stupid to learn to say Qasim?" asked Muhammad. "They've learned to say Chen and Giovani and Dubronski, haven't they?"

"This is where I get off, brothers," said Qasim with sarcasm. He then turned down a side street toward his house. Muhammad and Brian cut through the woods to their own neighborhood, leaving Daud at the street where he lived.

"Assalaamu alaykum*," said Daud. "See you, Brian."

"Wa alaykum assalaam**," said Muhammad.

"See you."

Just Muhammad and Brian continued walking.

Brian was very surprised by the exchange of words that had just taken place between the three other boys. The anger in it was completely unexpected. He knew that both Daud and Muhammad were Muslims and were proud of it. He hadn't known that Casey was a Muslim until the argument broke out.

"Do you remember when you first met me?" asked Muhammad suddenly.

"I guess so," said Brian. "Sure."

Muhammad was thinking that maybe he had been too hard on Qasim. "Was it difficult for you to say my name?"

Brian tried to remember back four years ago to when he first moved in. "I can't really remember that," he said. "I do know I'd never heard your name before or heard of Islam or anything."

"But was it a big deal to call me Muhammad?"

"No," said Brian. "It's just always been your name."

The boys continued walking for a minute.

---

* Peace be upon you, the Muslim greeting and goodbye.

** And upon you be peace, the answer to the Muslim greeting and goodbye.

"Do all your names have a meaning to them?" asked Brian.

"Almost all of them," said Muhammad.

"Yours is the name of your Prophet," said Brian.

"Yes," said Muhammad. "It also means the one who is praiseworthy."

"How about Daud?' asked Brian.

"He's named after the prophet David," said Muhammad.

"What about your brother, Jamaal?"

"Jamaal means the beautiful one. It's from one of the names of God."

"I don't know about your brother being beautiful," laughed Brian. "How about your sister, Fatima?"

"She's named after one of the Prophet's daughters."

"So, what about Casey?" asked Brian.

"His name's Qasim," said Muhammad. "It means the one who divides things into their proper portions."

Brian had never heard anything like that before. He thought of his own name and the names of people he knew.

"How come you got so angry?" he asked. "I mean, apart from him teasing you like that?"

"He's trading something with meaning for something with no meaning," said Muhammad. "He's denying who he is."

Brian just nodded, and then the boys separated to their homes.

"See you."

"See you."

Muhammad thought a lot about what had happened that day. Later that evening, when they were returning from the Isha* prayer at the mosque, Muhammad briefly told his father about the events of that afternoon. His father nodded.

"I'm afraid it's like father, like son," said Mr. Saeed. "I met his father when they first moved in, you know. Dr. Adam and I went over to welcome them to the community. The man didn't want anything to do with us. He seems to be successfully trying to forget he's Muslim, where he comes from, and everything else about his roots. He just kept saying, 'We're in America now', as if that cancelled everything to do with our religion and culture. He was acting more 'American' than any American I ever met."

"Maybe he arrived before the pilgrims," said Muhammad.

Mr. Saeed let the comment pass. "Names are very important," he said.

"I know," said Muhammad. He was thinking. "But let's say someone's a sincere Muslim. Let's say he isn't ashamed of his background, but he changes his name because it really is impossible for people to say."

---

* (E-Sha) A night prayer in congregation; one of five prayers a day for Muslims.

"No," said Mr. Saeed. "The argument doesn't hold water. People learn all kinds of names here. There's a million different kinds of names in America."

"I guess you're right," said Muhammad.

"Lots of Muslims have been killed because of their names," said Mr. Saeed. Muhammad looked at his father.

"In Albania and Bulgaria under the communists, Muslims were forced to change their names and give up their religion or be killed. Many of them changed their names and signed away their lands and were killed anyway. If you didn't change your name you were denied any legal status or protection. Way back in Czarist Russia, whenever the Russians conquered Muslim lands they always made the people change their names. They made them change their languages too. Today in what used to be the Muslim provinces of Russia you get people with names like Rahmananov. That comes from the name Abdul Rahman, but now it sounds Russian. Stalin, the dictator, knew the importance of names. He believed that if you changed people's names and languages you could control them. He did that all over the former U.S.S.R. It's true too. If you change people's names and language you change the way they see themselves and think about the world. That way you can take away people's cultures and religions and rule them more easily."

Muhammad had never heard of someone being killed just because of a name before. It seemed crazy. Then he thought that it wasn't just the name though. The fight was over the meaning behind the name. Why not just keep the meaning and change the name?

"Why couldn't you just keep your Islam or culture or whatever, and only change your name on the outside?" he asked.

"You could," said Mr. Saeed. "That wouldn't really work though. You'd give up a little piece of who you are, but the people who forced you wouldn't be satisfied. Remember, it's not just the name they're after. They would force the next change on you, and the next and the next, until there was nothing left of the original you. Your way of life would be gone. The conqueror always forces the conquered to imitate him. That's the ultimate victory."

"Nobody even needs to force Qasim to give up his name. He's doing it voluntarily."

"A lot of people are like that," Mr. Saeed said.

"I'd never give up my name," said Muhammad.

Mr. Saeed nodded. "You know, that's one of the rights a child has over his or her parents."

"What is?" asked Muhammad.

"The Prophet said that one of the rights a child has over its parent is to be given a good name."

"Who would give their child a bad name?"

Mr. Saeed smiled. "A boy came to the Prophet once complaining that his father had named him, Baby Chicken."

Muhammad laughed.

"It's true," said his father.

"I know," said Muhammad. "It just sounds so funny." He wondered what it would be like going through life with a name like, 'Baby Chicken'.

"The Prophet told us not to give each other degrading nicknames either," continued Mr. Saeed.

Muhammad knew about nicknames already, but he was still stuck thinking about 'Baby Chicken'. "Ladies and gentlemen, may I introduce to you the chairman of the board and Chief Executive Officer, Baby Chicken! ...and seated on my left is the noted professor of economics at Harvard University, Dr. Baby Chicken... Gentlemen, this crime has all the earmarks of that villain of darkness, Baby Chicken!" Muhammad couldn't help smiling at his thoughts. You probably wouldn't even get out of kindergarten alive with a name like that!

The next Saturday, Muhammad almost bowed out of the football game. He didn't really feel like having a confrontation with Qasim, and he thought the other boy might provoke one. In the end he went anyway rather than run from the situation.

Qasim's team won the coin toss and chose to receive the kickoff from Muhammad's team. Qasim was playing quarterback again. It wasn't even ten minutes into the game before he resumed calling Muhammad 'Mo'.

Muhammad was playing back, covering a boy from

Qasim's team as he went out to receive a pass. Qasim let fly a long pass, but Muhammad leapt into the air and knocked it down before the other boy could grab it.

"Yo, Mo!" shouted Qasim. "Nice block!" The compliment was actually meant as an insult because of the name. Muhammad managed to hold his temper, but he could see everyone on both teams watching him for his reaction.

"His whole team will start calling me that if I let him get away with it," Muhammad thought. "If he does it again, I'm going to have to do something."

The next play went without incident and then the ball changed sides. It took four plays, but Muhammad's team made a touchdown with Daud running the ball over the goal line. Muhammad's team kicked off and then Qasim's team had possession of the ball.

As the two teams were setting up across from each other to begin play, Qasim called out to the boy Muhammad was covering. "See if you can get rid of Mo there, and I'll pass you the ball, Ed."

Muhammad straightened up. He made his decision and then began to take a step, but Brian was already striding across the line toward the other team's quarterback, calling time out as he went. He quickly reached Qasim and with a smile on his face spoke through clenched teeth in a whisper.

"You stop calling him 'Mo'," he said. "You may not be

proud of being Muslim and where your parents come from, but he is; so call him Muhammad! Understand? He probably wouldn't fight you about it, but I definitely will, and I guarantee you, you'll lose!"

Still smiling, Brian patted the surprised boy on the shoulder. "No more Mo," he said. Then he turned back toward his own team. "Time in!" he called and strode back across the line. "The ball's in play!"

Qasim didn't say another word to Muhammad throughout the whole game.

The final score was closer this time, but Muhammad's team still lost. As the boys stood around waiting to head back home, Muhammad approached Brian.

"What did you say to him?" he asked.

Daud was crowding close too.

"I just reminded him of his manners," Brian said.

Qasim was waiting alone across the field for the three boys to leave before him. Brian glanced over at him. "You guys go ahead," he said. "I want to walk back with Casey."

Daud and Muhammad gave Brian puzzled looks, but didn't force the matter. Brian walked back to where Qasim was waiting. Qasim eyed him warily as he approached.

"Don't worry," said Brian. "I just want to walk back with you. Honest, nothing else."

"I'll fight you if you want," said Qasim defensively.

Brian laughed. "I used to get into fights when I first moved in here," he said, "but I haven't had a fight in over three years now. Come on."

Qasim looked relieved, but still upset. As the two boys walked along the road, he seemed to be puzzling over something.

"What would make you fight for him?" he finally asked.

"Because he stands up for what he believes in," said Brian. "He is what he is and he doesn't care what other people think. I respect him."

The boys continued in silence until they came to Qasim's street.

"I'll see you," said Qasim as he turned down the road. Then he added, "I'll see you in school."

"Sure thing," said Brian.

As he continued on, Brian glanced back at Qasim. Brian shook his head. People are funny, he thought. You force them to shape up and they either become your friend or your enemy. It looked like Casey might just become a friend. Brian shook his head again. People sure were funny.

Qasim was walking toward his house alone, contemplating his name. He was thinking that maybe it wasn't such a clumsy name after all. In all his years living in three different towns he couldn't think of one friend who would have stuck up for him like Brian had stuck up for Muhammad.

Respect; but it was respect for Muhammad's being different, not for his being the same. That was totally new for Qasim. It was exactly the opposite of how he and his family worked.

As he turned in at his driveway, Qasim wondered what the reaction would be at school if he changed his name back to the original. He wondered if he had the courage to do it. It could backfire. Then he thought about the other Muslims in school. He'd never really paid much attention to them before. He wondered what his parents would think.

"I don't know," he thought, as he went up his front steps. "I might just have to give it a try."

THE VANDALS

Muhammad hadn't been to the old clubhouse in almost a year. They called it a clubhouse, though it was really only a network of hollowed out bushes with a plywood roof built up inside the middle bush. It was on a small rise in the woods at the end of Muhammad's street and was well hidden if you didn't know the way in. A few years ago, before the new houses had been built, the woods had been much bigger and Muhammad and his friends had felt they owned the whole area. The clubhouse had been their fortress. From it they ruled their domain. Over the past two years though, Muhammad had stopped coming. He had begun to spend more time at the mosque, and playing basketball, or with other friends away from his own neighborhood. The woods just didn't feel like his anymore, not with all the new houses and streets that forced the stream to go down underground through a cement conduit, and all the new kids that now frequented his former kingdom. You could barely come into the woods now-a-days without seeing three or four other kids, some of them much older. Muhammad's friend, Daud, had moved into one of the new houses, but he was the only good thing the houses had brought.

As Muhammad and his friend, Brian, poked around the bushes, they could easily see the handiwork of some of the new arrivals to the neighborhood. One whole wall of the bushes had been broken out. Apparently, someone had wanted the plywood roof and the legs it stood on for another purpose. They had simply broken and cut away branches to get through to it. Looking inside, the old clubhouse was completely overgrown and choked with new branches.

"It's the end of an era," said Muhammad dramatically.

"Hey, look at this," said Brian. He was standing at the edge of the last trees where they met the field that used to go all the way to the stream. There was a road at the far end of the field now, and beyond that, the housing development that had ruined the woods. Cutting from the road into the field toward where the boys stood, was a new dirt road. Neither boy had seen it before. On either side of the dirt road new housing lots were staked out. The wooden stakes with their red strips of cloth stood out clearly against the thin straw and low tufts of dry grass.

"Oh, no," said Muhammad. "More of them."

Over the next three weeks the boys watched as construction started on six of the more than twenty lots. In the evenings, after the workers had left, they would come down from the woods into the field to check out the new construction.

"Man," said Brian. "They throw these things up fast!"

"Yeah," agreed Muhammad. "They have special crews for each part."

"I wish they had a crew to take them down again," said Brian.

Muhammad laughed.

The two boys were standing beside a house that had already been closed in with outside walls and the roof. Workers had been doing the roofing, and big buckets of liquid tar were lined up along the building.

Brian stepped between the buckets and rapped his knuckles against the plywood wall. "You could probably push it down," he said, though it sounded sturdy enough to Muhammad.

Muhammad wandered across the dirt road to another house which had just been framed-in the day before. It was interesting walking around inside the forest of upright two by fours, trying to figure out where exactly the rooms would be and each room's purpose. He stepped through the opening for the front door and jumped off the cement slab onto what would eventually be the front walkway and lawn. He could see where excavation had started for another group of houses. He crossed the dirt road again to see what Brian was doing.

"In another five years there won't be a tree left standing," he said as he rounded the corner of the closed-in house. Suddenly he stopped dead with a sinking feeling in his stomach.

"Brian," he said.

Brian stood holding a two foot stake with a rag tied around the top of it. The rag was covered with tar and Brian was just leaning over an open bucket dipping out more tar. On the

YANKEE
GO HOME

wall beside him he had written in big, black letters, "YANKEE GO HOME". He turned his head and smiled at Muhammad.

"What?" he said.

"That's wrong," said Muhammad, feeling kind of stupid as he said it.

"Come on," said Brian. "It's just a joke. They have to put that insulation stuff and the siding over it anyway. It doesn't hurt anybody." He added an exclamation mark and then dipped up more tar and started drawing a face.

Muhammad remembered another time Brian had told him something was just a joke. They had ridden their bikes over by the golf course and hidden them in the trees. They had lain down at the edge of the course like commandos watching the golfers teeing off and taking their shots until they finally got to the green and putted in their balls. They had made jokes about the ability and outfits of the different golfers and then Brian had said, "Watch this."

He timed it perfectly. A new group of three golfers had just gotten their balls close to the green. Brian burst onto the course at a full run. As he headed toward the green the golfers suddenly realized what was happening and started to run too, waving their clubs and shouting. Brian circled the green, picking up the three balls and headed back to the trees. Muhammad was standing now, watching as the two caddies swerved to cut Brian off before he hit the trees. It was going to be close. Then Brian had leapt into the trees past Muhammad, shouting, “Come on!”, and Muhammad was crashing through the trees behind him, with the caddies right behind them. They had reached their bikes and gotten going just before the two caddies burst out onto the road. “It’s only a joke,” Brian had said. Muhammad never went near the golf course with him again.

“You’re crazy,” said Muhammad. “I don’t want any part of this.”

Brian was adding eyes to the face he was drawing. He made them big circles with crossed pupils that looked like they were moving. Then he stepped back to view his handiwork and laughed.

Muhammad had to admit it looked funny. Suddenly he was laughing too. His nervousness made it all seem a lot funnier than it actually was. “You should put a mustache on it,” he said, before he realized what he was doing. Then a pang of regret hit him. “Listen,” he said. “I’m going.”

“All right,” said Brian. “Hold your horses and let me put this lid back on.”

Muhammad waited impatiently while Brian dropped his makeshift brush and pounded the lid of the tar bucket back in place. Some tar splattered out and Brian wiped the heel of his hand on a tuft of grass. As they entered the woods again, Muhammad didn’t look back at the house like Brian did. He was thinking that he was going to stop coming to the construction site, maybe even stop hanging around with Brian for a while. It had been stupid to keep coming down there anyhow. Muhammad figured there really wasn't any harm done though, Brian was right about that. The wall still had to be covered and a little tar wouldn't hurt it any. Muhammad just thanked Allah that they hadn't been caught.

"I'm not going back there any more," said Muhammad. "You shouldn't have done that. Getting into that kind of thing is wrong."

"Okay," said Brian. "It's no big deal."

That was the end of it, or so the boys thought.

"Did you see that new house they just finished on Sharrow Lane?" asked Mr. Saeed. It was one week later and the Saeed family was at the table eating dinner.

"No," said Mrs. Saeed.

"The whole thing's been vandalized," said Mr. Saeed. "All the windows have been smashed out and someone wrote with tar all across the front of the house. They wrote, 'Yankee go home', all over it."

Muhammad's blood ran cold and he almost dropped his fork. His mother was the only one who seemed to notice and looked at him strangely.

Muhammad barely got himself through the rest of the meal. He ate very little. As soon as he could, he excused himself. Checking to see that nobody was following him, he ran upstairs to his parent's room to telephone Brian. He quietly closed the door and dialed the phone. Muhammad had the uneasy feeling that his mother had been staring at him all through dinner.

"Brian?"

"Yes," came the reply.

"Did you vandalize that house again?"

"What?"

Muhammad was talking in a nervous whisper. "I said, did you vandalize that house again?"

"What are you talking about, vandalize?" Brian was angry now.

"Someone smashed out all the windows and wrote all over it in tar."

"So, what are you calling me for?" Brian said.

"It said, 'Yankee go home'," said Muhammad.

There was a silence at the end of the line.

Then Brian said in a flat voice, "I didn't do it."

There was a long silence again. Muhammad wasn't sure he believed his friend. He didn't know what to say.

"I've got to hang up," said Brian and the line went dead.

As Muhammad was replacing the phone, Mrs. Saeed came into the room.

"Who were you talking to?" she asked.

"Oh, just Brian," said Muhammad a little too quickly.

Mrs. Saeed stood in the doorway evaluating her son. Then she closed the door.

"You had tar splatters on your trousers last weekend," she said. "I saw it when I did the laundry. And I know you've been visiting the construction site."

Muhammad felt a sudden cringing in his arms and chest. The feeling rose straight up to his face and flooded it with heat. He just waited, powerless, without moving.

"Did you have anything to do with that vandalism?" his mother asked. Her voice was very thin and controlled. She was waiting too, and she looked afraid; very steady, but afraid. It was like time was suspended for a moment. Both mother and son stood, gazing out at the edge of something awful.

"No," said Muhammad finally.

Mrs. Saeed remained looking at her son. Something was wrong and she knew it. They both felt it.

"Are you sure?" asked Mrs. Saeed, giving her son another chance. She was really asking, "Are you sure you want to give me that answer?" She didn't think he would have done the vandalism, but she knew there was something really wrong. She could see it in him now, she had seen it all through dinner.

"I didn't do it," said Muhammad, and it was the truth, but it wasn't the whole truth. What he did do, or took part in, along with his doubt about Brian and his mother's doubt about him, all combined to make his words seem hollow, paper thin. They felt like a lie. He kept thinking how it must look to her.

"You know," said his mother. "You can tell me anything. Whether you did it or you didn't do it, you can tell me anything."

It was the first time real distrust had ever entered their relationship. It was like a poisonous snake silently appearing between them.

"I know that," said Muhammad. "I didn't do anything."

An hour later the police arrived.

Mr. Saeed let the officers in and he and Mrs. Saeed and Muhammad sat with them downstairs. Jamaal and Fatima were told to wait upstairs, but from where he was sitting, Muhammad could see them sneaking down the stairway to peek and listen.

"I didn't do it," Muhammad repeated.

"We have a witness who saw you and your friend from across the street putting tar on the same house last weekend. Mr. Davis, the builder, notified us and he wants to press charges."

"I didn't put any tar on the house," said Muhammad.

"But you were there," said Mr. Saeed.

"Yes," said Muhammad.

"And you didn't stop it," said Mr. Saeed.

"The second act of vandalism was done exactly like the first one," said the first policeman.

"I never touched the house that second time!"

"Just the first time," said the second policeman.

"I never touched it any time!" said Muhammad in exasperation.

"All right," said the first officer, standing up. "In any case, we want you down at the police station first thing in the morning. You're a minor, so your father can bring you." Now he spoke to Mr. Saeed. "Mr. Davis is coming down to make a formal complaint before he leaves for the job site in the morning. You'd better be at the station by eight o'clock. If you're not, we'll have to send a squad car to pick up your son."

As soon as the policemen left, Mr. Saeed started to put his coat on. "Get your jacket," he said to Muhammad.

"Where are we going?" asked Muhammad.

"Just get your jacket on."

As Muhammad was leaving he turned and looked at his mother. She was standing in the living room with one arm crossing her stomach and grasping her other arm at the elbow. She looked defeated. Muhammad suddenly felt like crying.

"I didn't do it, mom," he said, and then he was out the door, running to catch his father.

THE VANDALS II

Mr. Saeed and Muhammad spent an hour at Brian's house with Brian and his father, going over everything. The boys told their story. Muhammad still wasn't really sure Brian hadn't done it. That made Brian unsure of Muhammad and both parents seemed unsure of the other's son and even unsure of their own. It was like an overgrown thicket of distrust. Where there had been perfect trust before, there were now only shadows and doubts. Muhammad couldn't figure a way out of it. He didn't even know exactly how they'd gotten there. Still, the two fathers decided on a plan of action.

After trying many times, Mr. Saeed finally got Mr. Davis on the telephone. It took twenty minutes of apologizing, arguing and coaxing before Mr. Davis finally agreed to see them.

"Two thousand dollars!" said Mr. Davis roughly. "More than that with the labor! I'm not a big company. What I got I built with my own two hands, and it makes me sick to see hard work trashed for some mindless kick!"

"They didn't do it," repeated Brian's father.

"So you've been telling me," said Mr. Davis. "But I've got a witness. He saw what they did last weekend. He was out walking his dog. He called me today when he saw that they'd done it again last night."

"They've already admitted to last weekend," said Mr. Saeed.

Muhammad looked at Brian. At least Brian had been decent enough to say that Muhammad hadn't touched the house; for all the good it did.

"Look," said Mr. Saeed. "We'll make good your losses, to the penny."

"And it won't make your insurance rates go up by claiming it from your insurance company," added Brian's father.

"Sure," said Mr. Davis. "And your kids get off scott free!"

"We don't want them to get off free," said Mr. Saeed. "Because they did do it the first time, they'll have to repay us every cent. We don't want them to pay with a police record for something they didn't do, however."

"Hah!" grunted Mr. Davis. "It's not good enough. Buying your way out of trouble doesn't cut it in my book."

"How about if they also work it off?" asked Mr. Saeed. "Say, they work for six months, weekends and some days after school."

"I don't want them working for me!" said Mr. Davis.

"Think about it," said Brian's father. "You could make them work as hard as you want."

"Yeah," thought Mr. Davis to himself. "I'd work them all right! I'd make them sweat for their mistakes!"

"Nah," he said after thinking. "I couldn't take the liability."

"No liability," said Mr. Saeed. "We'll sign it if you want."

Mr. Davis looked at the two boys again. They had more than he'd ever had as a kid, and they thought they could go around destroying property. He could work that out of them! He'd teach them what it was like to have to build something rather than just destroy it. "Let me see your hands," he said.

The two boys looked at their fathers and then one after the other held out their hands, palms up. Mr. Davis reached across and took one set of hands in his own hands, rubbing the soft palms with his hard, coarse thumbs. Then he took the other set. Baby hands! Mr. Davis pictured the boys carrying bricks and wheeling barrows of cement, then shoveling dirt. He dropped the last set of hands.

Muhammad and Brian looked at each other. They weren't so sure about this solution. Mr. Davis' hands had felt like they were big lumps of wood, thinly covered in flesh. After all, they hadn't even done what they were being accused of doing.

Mr. Davis sat back in his chair. "All right," he said. "It's a deal. And I work seven days a week, Saturdays and Sundays. They get no weekends except with me!"

Mrs. Saeed was still sitting alone in the living room. Earlier she had settled Fatima and Jamaal back into bed and finally calmed them to sleep.

"Is Muhammad going to jail?" Jamaal had asked.

"No," said Mrs. Saeed.

"Where did he and daddy go?"

"I don't know," said Mrs. Saeed. "I think they went to see someone."

"Did Muhammad do what the policemen said?" asked Fatima.

"No," said Mrs. Saeed, but she wished she was sure in her own heart. Up till that evening she would have staked her life on the knowledge that Muhammad would never lie to her. "Go to sleep," she said. "You have school tomorrow."

Now, as she sat in the chair in the living room, she thought about Muhammad when he was a baby, when he had been her only baby. She passed from one memory to another through the years of his growing up. She couldn't remember his ever having lied to her. Oh, there were the little denials when he was really small, but since he'd been old enough to understand, he had never lied to her. She was sure of that, or was she? Then, what about willful destruction? He said he hadn't done it, but he acted like he had. Mrs. Saeed remembered the tar on Muhammad's pants. Then she remembered his behavior at dinner and afterwards when she'd asked him about the tar. She remembered the hushed, secret phone call to Brian she had interrupted. He had acted guilty and she had known it and he had known she knew. She had seen it all in his eyes. It was amazing how years of trust could just turn to nothing in one evening.

Mrs. Saeed wiped the tears from her cheeks and as she did so, suddenly became very angry. How dare he destroy that trust? How dare he? She was angry at herself then too, for letting him do it. She was suddenly so angry, she stood up and began pacing around the room. How could he destroy their trust like that, and she just let it happen; crying over it in a chair, just letting it happen!

Mrs. Saeed went into the kitchen and put some water on to boil for tea.

"I have to think clearly about this," she thought. "Crying is no solution, and getting angry is no solution. I have to repair what's happened."

She watched the kettle and thought. Muhammad had done something wrong, whether little or big, still had to be ascertained. Not just wrong, but criminal, Mrs. Saeed corrected herself. He had also lied to her or not lied. At that, Mrs. Saeed's heart wrenched inside her because she was sure he had lied, or at least not told the truth. In any case, a poison had gotten into their family.

"We have to extract the poison and heal the wound without leaving the family scarred," she thought. "No, there has to be just enough of a scar to always remind Muhammad. He should never forget this. There should never be a next time."

When Mr. Saeed and Muhammad came home almost an hour later, they found Mrs. Saeed calmly sitting in the same living room chair.

"We have to talk," she said.

As Muhammad sat down he noticed that his mother looked very different from when he'd left.

"Mom," said Muhammad, but Mrs. Saeed put up her hand and stopped him from speaking.

"I don't want you to say anything tonight," said Mrs. Saeed. "I don't want any denials, true or untrue. I just want you to think. I want you to think about what you brought into this house and understand exactly what brought it here. We will talk tomorrow."

Mr. and Mrs. Saeed watched Muhammad go upstairs.

"Mr. Davis is going to allow us to pay for the damages and he won't press charges," said Mr. Saeed. "Both Muhammad and Brian will work weekends on his construction site as a punishment. They didn't do it," he added, "not the second time anyway. I'm pretty sure of that. Still, we're stuck with it. Mr. Alexander was out walking his dog when he saw them the first time. The police would never believe the second time wasn't them too."

"What about Brian?" asked Mrs. Saeed.

"I don't know," said Mr. Saeed. "I don't think he did the

second one, but I can't be sure. He confessed to doing it the first time, and he freely admitted that Muhammad didn't touch the house. He didn't have to admit that."

"But Muhammad was with him," said Mrs. Saeed.

"Yes," answered Mr. Saeed. "He was watching."

"That makes him part of it," said Mrs. Saeed. "He at least took part by being there and not stopping it." Then Mrs. Saeed went on to tell her husband about the tar on Muhammad's clothes and their conversation after dinner.

"We'll see what he comes up with when we speak to him tomorrow," said Mr. Saeed.

"The truth, I hope," said Mrs. Saeed. "I don't want him to make any excuses to himself. I can't bear to think he can't be trusted."

Mr. Saeed sighed. "He'll be all right," he said. "Growing up isn't easy."

"No," said Mrs. Saeed. "I know it isn't."

Upstairs in his room, Muhammad lay awake thinking.

If only he hadn't hung around with that crazy Brian, it was all his fault! Or that Mr. Alexander and his dog; they didn't do anything, and he thought it was them and the police thought it was them, and his parents even thought it was them, and all because of Brian! Why couldn't his parents trust him? What did they think he was, a lying thief?

Muhammad ranted and raved in his mind against

everybody, but in the back of his consciousness was the memory of his own words, "You should put a mustache on it." In the back of his mind he knew he was not completely guiltless. In the car, his father had said to him, "Allah does not wrong people, people wrong themselves."

"But I didn't have anything to do with the vandalism," Muhammad had said. "I didn't even do it the first time!"

"If you graze your sheep near the fence, they are bound to go over," Mr. Saeed had replied. "If you play near the forbidden, you are bound to fall into it."

"But I didn't touch that house!" said Muhammad.

"Understand what I'm saying," said Mr. Saeed. "Are you completely blameless in all this?"

Muhammad wanted to yell "Yes!" but he had held his tongue.

Now, as he punched his fist into the pillow on his bed, he hissed, "Stupid! Stupid, stupid, stupid!" One sentence of his own words made him guilty. He should have just walked away as soon as he saw what Brian was doing. Or he should have stopped him, just physically stopped him. They shouldn't have been playing around in the construction anyway. Now he'd have to give every penny he got, almost forever, to his dad just to pay back the damages! And he didn't even do it! Muhammad remembered the gleam he had seen in Mr. Davis' eyes when he realized he could work the boys to death without any objection.

Every weekend!

Muhammad sat up and switched on the light. His little brother, Jamaal was sleeping soundly across the room. Muhammad went to the bookcase and took out a copy of the Quran*. He spent the next hour reading the translation, flipping here and there through the pages, looking for something to get him off the hook. Again and again, the message that seemed to come out to him was, don't blame anyone else for your troubles, set yourself straight first. Muhammad sighed and closed the Quran. He placed it back in the bookcase and turned out the light.

The next day at school Muhammad thought about his problem again and again. He was not guilty of the actions he was being blamed for but he was guilty of some other things, small things. Well, maybe they weren't such small things in the sight of Allah. They had certainly blown up into a huge amount of trouble for him. He spent the day trying to separate everything out and still dreaded having to talk to his parents when he got home. He dreaded more the possibility of things not getting cleared up though, of his parents not trusting what he said, always wondering and asking what he was really up to.

When Muhammad got home, his father's car was already in the driveway, which was unusual. Muhammad had a sudden

---

* The Muslim Holy Book.

fear that something else had happened. Probably the police had found some vandalism twenty miles away and were blaming him for it! Instead, Mr. Saeed had just come home early so they could talk.

After making Muhammad's brother and sister a snack and then sending them upstairs to do their homework, Muhammad and his parents sat down in the living room. Muhammad started with some embarrassment and went through the whole story. He left nothing out and even went over the dinner yesterday and his conversation with his mother afterwards.

"So, what's your analysis?" asked Mr. Saeed.

Muhammad had thought a lot about that. "I didn't do the vandalism the second time," he said. "There I'm being blamed for something I didn't have anything to do with. The reason I'm being blamed is partially my fault though.

"I shouldn't have been playing at the construction site, and I should have stopped Brian as soon as I saw what he was doing. Then, I should have told you the whole story, mom, when we were in your bedroom. It just seemed simpler to flatly deny the vandalism, which was the truth, than to go through a lengthy explanation. Without the explanation though, it left all this mistrust. I guess that's what I did wrong, and I'm sorry. I really am sorry about it."

"What about Brian as a friend?" asked Mr. Saeed.

"Yeah, I don't know," said Muhammad. "I'll have to see if this has changed him. He did stick up for me last night though."

"I guess that's fair enough," said Mr. Saeed.

"I want you to see all of this clearly," said Mrs. Saeed. "The part of it that is your responsibility, I want you to take complete responsibility for. I want you to understand that and change. We are all answerable. And lastly, I don't ever want you to lie to me, or tell me a partial truth again. Ever."

"You'd better get your homework done," said Mr. Saeed. "You're going to be working this weekend."

The first day of work was even worse than Muhammad thought it would be. He and Brian felt used just like donkeys. They had to unload trucks and move bricks. They had to shift bags of cement around in the wheelbarrow to where they were needed. For the last few hours of the day Mr. Davis had them digging a trench, even though there was a backhoe sitting idle on one of the other lots. When the two boys dragged themselves home at six o'clock, they could hardly walk. Muhammad's legs, back and arms all ached and his hands were covered with blisters.

"You'd better get into a hot bath and soak off some of that dirt and keep yourself from getting stiff," said Mrs. Saeed. After Muhammad emerged from the bath, she took a look at his hands.

Some of the blisters were puffed up like balloons, but

some were already broken. They were really sore. Mrs. Saeed put disinfectant on the open ones which made Muhammad jump and squirm. Then she covered them with band aids. "You're lucky you got caught," was all she said. "Pretty soon these will all be callouses. It's better to have callouses on your hands than on your heart."

Muhammad didn't feel hungry after his bath, he felt like going straight to bed, but at dinner he found himself eating a lot. After the sunset prayer his father drove him to the mall to buy some work gloves. Muhammad was so tired, it all felt like a dream. When they got home, he did his night prayer and went straight to bed.

The next three weeks were much the same, but after a month, Muhammad felt stronger and his hands had grown hard. He still ached, but the work did not drive him into the ground. Another thing had changed about the work. Muhammad was learning something about masonry. He'd spent all the previous weekend as a bricklayer's aid. The chance to learn something suddenly made the job a whole lot more interesting.

One night Muhammad was sitting up in his room, copying something out of a book in Arabic, using a felt tip pen. Jamaal was sitting on his bed, playing with some toy cars. Muhammad finished the Arabic writing and wrote the English translation underneath. Both jobs took a long time. When he was done, he got some tape from his desk drawer and taped the paper up on the wall over his bed. He stepped back to study the result.

The sign read, “Both permitted and forbidden things are evident but in between them there are doubtful things and most of the people have no knowledge about them. So whoever saves himself from these doubtful things saves his religion and his honor. And whoever indulges in these doubtful things is like a shepherd who grazes near the private pasture of someone else and at any moment he is liable to get into it. Beware, every king has a private pasture and the private pasture of Allah on the earth is His forbidden things. Beware! There is a piece of flesh in the body, if it becomes good the whole body becomes good, but if it gets spoiled the whole body gets spoiled, and that is the heart.”

“What’s that?” asked Jamaal.

“It’s a hadith,” said Muhammad.

“No, I mean what is it?”

“That, my boy, is the difference between the Fire and the Garden,” said Muhammad dramatically. “That is the difference between breaking your back every weekend hauling bricks or playing basketball with your friends.”

Two days later, while Muhammad was upstairs soaking in a bath after work, Mr. Davis came to the door. Muhammad dressed and got downstairs as fast as he could. When he entered the living room, his whole family was there and his parents were talking earnestly with Mr. Davis. “Oh, no,” thought Muhammad.

"What now?"

Mr. Davis stood as Muhammad came in and offered his hand. When they shook hands, Mr. Davis turned Muhammad's hand palm upward and ran his thumb across the surface. "It's a different hand now," he commented.

Muhammad sat down somewhat bewildered.

Mr. Davis also sat and came right to the point.

"They've caught the vandals," he said. "The police caught them last night in that new development out on route 40. They confessed to a whole string of vandalism, including my project. They're a bunch of kids who go to Avery High School so they pass by my houses every day. Apparently, they saw your 'YANKEE GO HOME' and decided to use it to put your signature on their work. I owe you and Brian an apology."

"That's all right," said Muhammad. "I know what it looked like, and we did do it the first time."

Both Muhammad's parents noticed that Muhammad said "we". He was including himself in the act.

"Anyway", said Mr. Davis, reaching into his inside jacket pocket. "I not only owe you an apology, I also owe your father some money." He took out two checks and handed one to Mr. Saeed. "One thousand, three hundred, seventeen dollars and seventy-two cents," he said. Then he looked down at the other check.

"This one's for ninety hours of work, including today."

He held the check out to Muhammad. "I gave you minimum wage."

The check was for four hundred, twenty-seven dollars and fifty cents. Muhammad had never had that much money before.

"You're a good worker," said Mr. Davis as he stood to go.

"Won't you stay and have some tea?" asked Mrs. Saeed.

"No, I'm afraid I have to get next door and apologize to the Deckers too," said Mr. Davis.

As he stood at the front door, ready to leave, he shook hands again with Mr. Saeed. Then he shook hands with Muhammad. "You'll be able to sleep late tomorrow," he said. "In a couple of years though, if you need a summer job or part time work, just look me up. You'll always have a place."

As Muhammad closed the door, he thought about the handshake. His hand was almost as hard as Mr. Davis' now. He looked at his palm and rubbed his thumb across the callouses. His hands would turn soft again. "Never mind," he thought. "I can make them hard again, maybe in a couple of years."

THE GUEST

Uncle Anwar's friend was coming to visit. His name was Abdul Jabbar and he had just arrived from Pakistan. He had called Mr. Saeed on the telephone to say he was on his way.

"I'm at Kennedy Airport in New York," he had said over a line filled with background noise. "Your brother, Anwar, is my boon companion and most respected friend. I have a letter of introduction."

Mr. Saeed racked his brain for any friend of his brother's who was named Abdul Jabbar. He couldn't think of any. If he was Anwar's "boon companion and most respected friend", Mr. Saeed was sure he would know him. He knew all of his younger brother's best friends. Never mind, maybe the man was exaggerating a little about the closeness of the friendship. Mr. Saeed was sure the letter of introduction from his brother would explain everything.

Mr. Saeed was about to invite Abdul Jabbar to come visit them when he left New York, but Abdul Jabbar invited himself first.

"I'm coming to you by bus," he said. "Can you meet me at the bus station?" He was shouting into the phone over the noise at the airport.

"New York's a long way from here," said Mr. Saeed.

"What bus will you be on?"

"What?" shouted Abdul Jabbar.

"I said, what bus will you be on!" repeated Mr. Saeed loudly. "When should I meet you?"

"What?"

"When should I meet you?"

"Then I should greet you, too!" shouted back Abdul Jabbar.

"No . . ." said Mr. Saeed.

"Yes, go!" said Abdul Jabbar, and the line went dead.

Mr. Saeed held the phone receiver away from his ear and stared at it.

"But how can we meet him if we don't know when he's arriving?" asked Muhammad, after his father had explained the phone call.

"We can't," said Mr. Saeed. "He'll have to call again when he arrives at the station."

"What's a 'boom companion'?" asked Jamaal.

"Boon companion, honey," said Mrs. Saeed.

"Okay, boon companion," repeated Jamaal.

"It's a friend," said Fatima.

"It's a best friend," said Mr. Saeed. "I don't remember anyone named Abdul Jabbar, though."

"Maybe he's a friend from your brother's new job," suggested Mrs. Saeed.

"That's possible," said Mr. Saeed. "I haven't been to Pakistan since Anwar took the new job. Abdul Jabbar must be a new friend. Anyway," he continued, speaking to the children, "he is going to be our guest for a few days and we must all treat him with the respect and service that a guest is due."

"He has a right to three full days of hospitality, but anything beyond that is our choice and charity," said Muhammad, paraphrasing the Prophet Muhammad.

"That's right," said Mr. Saeed. "And remember, serving the guest is one of the highest things you can do in Islam."

"You should also remember that Abdul Jabbar is from a different country," said Mrs. Saeed. "He may have different habits than you're used to. He may seem a little strange to you children at first, so you will just have to be patient."

"That's right," said Mr. Saeed. "We must all just remember he's our guest."

"Hello?"

"Hello?"

"Hello?" Mr. Saeed was lying in bed with the phone to his ear. It was pitch dark and he was not quite awake. He glanced at the luminous clock. It was two a.m. "Who is this?" He asked, and then he realized who it must be. "Abdul Jabbar?"

"Yes," said the voice over the phone. "Where are you?"

"I'm . . . I'm in bed," said Mr. Saeed, surprised.

"It's very late," said the voice.

Mr. Saeed cleared his throat and pushed himself into a sitting position.

"Why didn't you meet me?" Abdul Jabbar continued.

"Well, I . . ."

"It's very late!"

"Why, yes . . . yes, it is very late." Mr Saeed glanced at the clock. He wondered if he was dreaming.

"Where are you?" continued Abdul Jabbar.

Mr. Saeed had the strange feeling of going around in circles. "Where are you?" he said. "Are you at the station?"

There was a pause for a moment. It sounded like a hand was put over the receiver. "Yes," came Abdul Jabbar's voice eventually. "Yes, I am."

Mr. Saeed really did almost feel like he was dreaming. He ran a hand through his disheveled hair. "Abdul Jabbar."

"Yes."

"Can you see the big clock over the main door?"

"Yes," said Abdul Jabbar.

"God willing, I will meet you there in half an hour."

"Good," said Abdul Jabbar, and the line went dead.

When Mr. Saeed was dressed he felt more awake. He wondered if the telephone conversation had actually been as strange as it seemed. Probably not. No matter, he had to get to the bus station.

As Mr. Saeed pulled up to the station, he noticed a tall, thin man standing just inside the big glass doors. The man had a large suitcase and a shoulder bag on the floor beside him. He was wearing a dark suit whose pants and sleeves were much too short for him. He looked like an over-aged basketball player who had put on his grandson's suit by mistake.

"Abdul Jabbar?" asked Mr. Saeed, as he walked through the glass doors.

"Assalaamu alaykum!" said Abdul Jabbar. He bent down to give Mr. Saeed a big bear hug. He hugged Mr. Saeed hard and then he let go.

"Wa alaykum assalaam." said Mr. Saeed. He felt half crushed.

"You look just like your brother!" exclaimed Abdul Jabbar. "I would know you anywhere!"

Mr. Saeed was surprised. His brother, Anwar, was short, fat and bald. The two brothers could hardly look more different. "He's just being polite," thought Mr. Saeed.

Abdul Jabbar smiled broadly. He was beaming down at Mr. Saeed, but he looked terribly tired. His suit was all wrinkled, and he had dark circles under his eyes. His salt and pepper hair was sticking out in all directions. For an instant that long, unshaven face looked very familiar, but Mr. Saeed couldn't quite place it. For an instant, that face also looked slightly, well, crazy. "But flying like that, around the clock through different time zones, doesn't make anyone look good," thought Mr. Saeed.

"You must be tired," he said, as he bent to pick up Abdul Jabbar's suitcase. Then he added, "It's very late," and immediately shook his head. What did I say that for? He strained to lift the suitcase. It was very heavy! He used both hands but could barely lift it off the ground.

"I never get tired!" said Abdul Jabbar. "I am so excited to visit America and finally greet you in the flush!"

"Flesh," said Mr. Said.

"What?" said Abdul Jabbar.

"In the flesh," said Mr. Said.

"Precisely," said Abdul Jabbar.

"It's very late," thought Mr. Saeed. "Come," he said. "My car is right here."

Mr. Saeed dragged the huge suitcase to his car and opened the passenger door for Abdul Jabbar. Then he dragged the suitcase behind the car and heaved it into the trunk. The back of the car bounced up and down like a toy.

By the time Mr. Saeed reached the driver's seat, Abdul Jabbar was already asleep and snoring loudly. Through the whole drive home, he kept sliding sideways, down onto Mr. Saeed's shoulder. Mr. Saeed finally gave up pushing his limp body back into a sitting position and just left him leaning heavily on his shoulder, rasping decibels into his ear.

"Those long flights and bus rides are terrible," thought Mr. Saeed. He glanced at the sleeping face on his shoulder. He had the uncanny feeling that he knew Abdul Jabbar from somewhere. Could he actually have forgotten one of his brother's best friends? Mr. Saeed was sure the introduction letter would explain everything.

When they reached the house, Abdul Jabbar awoke miraculously. He followed Mr. Saeed who stumbled up the walkway under the weight of the immense suitcase. When Mr. Saeed opened the door and showed him in, Abdul Jabbar threw open his arms. "What a beautiful house!" he exclaimed. "I didn't eat dinner!"

"What?" asked Mr. Saeed.

"I didn't eat dinner!"

Mr. Saeed, put down the suitcase. "Of course," he said. He had planned on offering Abdul Jabbar something to eat after he showed him his room.

"Are you hungry?"

"Burgers!" exclaimed Abdul Jabbar. He gave a beaming, red-eyed, but winning smile.

"Burgers?"

"Burgers!"

"Burgers," said Mr. Saeed.

"Precisely," said Abdul Jabbar.

"It's late," said Mr. Saeed in a testing manner.

"It's very late!" said Abdul Jabbar.

Mr. Saeed paused. There was no way around it, the man seemed . . . not altogether normal. Differences in culture were one thing, but this man didn't act anything like a normal Pakistani would act. There was none of the extreme politeness, none of the self-effacement that a normal guest would be at pains to display. In fact, although Abdul Jabbar did seem completely harmless, at best one would have to say he was unbalanced. Was it possible that he was really one of Anwar's friends? But if not, how did he get our phone number? How does he know my brother? Mr. Saeed was quickly weighing probabilities. He felt caught between his duty as a host and the very real possibility that this man was an imposter or even dangerously insane. If the man was an imposter or dangerous, there was certainly no duty to host him for three minutes, much less three days.

"Do you have that letter from my brother?" he asked.

"Of course!" said Abdul Jabbar. "It's right in here." He dragged his suitcase across the room and flopped it down in the middle of the floor. He took a long time unzipping it and then began rummaging around inside, spilling clothes everywhere. Mr. Saeed couldn't believe his eyes, but he was sure he caught a glimpse of bricks at the bottom.

"Let me see, now where did I put that?" mumbled Abdul Jabbar. He had a bunch of envelopes in his hand and was sorting through them. Suddenly he stopped and struck the palm of his hand against his forehead like a bad actor. "Oh, no!" he exclaimed. He turned a pair of mournful eyes up toward Mr. Saeed. "I left it in the bus station! I had your telephone number written on it."

"I see!" said Mr. Saeed, who was now sure he had a slightly demented con-artist on his hands. "How did you get my brother's name and my phone number?" he demanded.

"Why, I told you . . ."

"Yes, I know, come on, pack up those things!"

"But, respected elder brother . . ."

Elder brother indeed! The man was old enough to be Mr. Saeed's father!

"I'm taking you back to the bus station," said Mr. Saeed.

"There's been some mistake," said Abdul Jabbar.

"Yes," said Mr. Saeed. "And it's late, too, isn't it?"

"Yes," said Abdul Jabbar, suddenly beaming. "It's very late!"

By now Mrs. Saeed was standing at the top of the stairs, looking down into the living room. She had a long robe and a scarf on. Muhammad was standing beside her, and Fatima and Jamaal had come out too.

Abdul Jabbar was wildly stuffing things back into his suitcase with Mr. Saeed standing over him.

"I told you, elder brother . . . I had the letter direct from your brother, Anwar. He handed it to me right under the big shade tree at the entrance to his courtyard. He forgot it in the house and sent his son, 'Choti Adami', to get it for me."

Mr. Saeed was suddenly filled with doubt. "Choti Adami" was the nick name of his brother's youngest son. It meant "little man". His brother's house did have a shade tree in front of the courtyard entrance, and it was his brother's habit to sit under it.

"How many son's does my brother have?" asked Mr. Saeed.

"Why, he has three sons and two daughters," answered Abdul Jabbar, in an injured tone, suddenly packing slowly, "though his eldest daughter, Rehana, is now recently married and living in Lahore, so that she is not at home, though she still receives mail there from her college friends, due to her recent change of address, which is all rather surprising in terms of your being some years older than your brother, where as you have only three children of a younger age to his more and older, but which can be explained by your leaving to work in America and late marriage, which, although odd, nonetheless never lessens your brother's love for you, and is apparent also in your love for him through so dutifully writing once a month your news, which of late, has changed to telephoning since he has had a telephone installed at number twelve, Thirteenth Street, New Town, way in the back, behind the railroad colony, where he's built a new addition since starting as chief engineer at the Famous Sugar Mill."

Mr. Saeed was struck silent by the onslaught of information. He had never heard such a sentence before in his life, and all in one breath! But it was true. It was all true! He glanced at his family and felt himself blush. He suddenly felt he had failed in his duty as a host. It was obvious that Abdul Jabbar knew Mr. Saeed's brother very well . . . But wait a minute, what about the bricks? Abdul Jabbar could actually be dangerous . . . Why would someone carry bricks around in his suitcase?

"What about those bricks?" asked Mr. Saeed.

"Oh," said Abdul Jabbar, beaming again. "A good idea, huh? The airline said there was a forty kilogram weight limit for baggage, but my clothes were just too light. Now my bag is forty kilos exactly! I'd let you have one, but I'll need them all for the return flight."

Well, that settled it. Abdul Jabbar was crazy all right, but not dangerous. He certainly knew Mr. Saeed's brother, Anwar, well. Mr. Saeed didn't see how he could refuse Abdul Jabbar his hospitality now. First, he was a guest and so was entitled to a three day stay. Second, at the very least he was extremely eccentric and Mr. Saeed wouldn't feel right putting him out on the street in a strange country. There was no telling what might happen to him. Third, this was a mystery that needed solving. Who exactly was this guy? What relation could he possibly have to Anwar? How did he even get into the country?

"I'm sorry," said Mr. Saeed.

"What?" said Abdul Jabbar.

"I apologize."

"I should hope so," said Abdul Jabbar, "but, no doubt, you are of a suspicious nature." He zipped closed his suitcase and stood up, "Your brother will be happy to hear that you are healthy in any case . . . And you look so much like him, elder brother!"

Mr. Saeed sighed. He supposed he would be "elder brother" for the rest of the visit. "No, I mean you're welcome to stay with us," said Mr. Saeed. "Please, stay. I apologize."

Mr. Saeed could see it was going to be a difficult, unpredictable three days, but he felt determined to give his guest his due.

Abdul Jabbar gave Mr. Saeed a big hug and was soon sprawled comfortably upon the couch. After introductions, the children were put back to bed. Mrs. Saeed insisted on making dinner for their guest. She didn't usually cook dinner at three a.m., but she felt embarrassed for her husband and wanted to help make up for it.

"I'm not sure exactly what we have," she said as she came downstairs and passed through to the kitchen.

"Burgers!" said Abdul Jabbar.

"Burgers?" asked Mrs. Saeed. She glanced at her

husband.

"Burgers," said Mr. Saeed.

"Precisely."

Mrs. Saeed defrosted some chopped meat and made two large hamburgers for the guest. After the meal was cooked and served she returned to bed.

Abdul Jabbar had been talking nonstop in seemingly endless sentences right up until his meal was served. Suddenly he became silent.

"What's this?" he asked.

"Burgers," said Mr. Saeed.

"So, this is what Americans eat?" said Abdul Jabbar with wonder. He picked up one hamburger, sniffed at it and ventured a small bite. His face became very long and he chewed slowly. He seemed to chew forever. He swallowed with difficulty. He glanced at his host and a smile spread across his face. "Excellent!" he exclaimed. He clapped his hands together. "Well, I'm exhausted, time for bed!" He leaned close to Mr. Saeed in a conspiratorial manner and said in a near whisper, "It's very late, you know."

Mr. Saeed nodded with his mouth partway open, and wondered what he'd gotten himself into.

After dragging Abdul Jabbar's suitcase downstairs and setting him up in the guest room, Mr. Saeed dragged himself upstairs and flopped into bed. He glanced at the clock. Abdul

Jabbar was right!

The next morning, at dawn, the whole Saeed family got up for the Fajr prayer. Unfortunately, it was less than an hour after Mr. Saeed had gone to bed. Mr. Saeed went down to the guest room and knocked on the door. "Abdul Jabbar," he called. "It's Fajr time." There was no answer. Mr. Saeed knocked again. "Abdul Jabbar . . ." After the third knock without any answer Mr. Saeed just let his guest sleep. Knocking three times and leaving if there was no answer was a practice of the Prophet. "He's too tired from jet-lag," thought Mr. Saeed. "He'll have to make up his prayer later."

After the prayer, everyone went back to bed. They would sleep for two hours more before getting up for the day. As Mr. Saeed went to sleep he was thinking that he would call his brother as soon as he woke up and find out who exactly Abdul Jabbar was and what to do with him.

In his sleep, Mr. Saeed dreamed about Pakistan. He and his brother, Anwar, were both young boys and they were walking along the road to their house. Abdul Jabbar kept passing them by, riding a bicycle. He passed them once, twice, and a third time, each time saying, "It certainly is late!" Mr. Saeed kept thinking, "I should know that guy." He asked his brother who he was, but Anwar just said, "I don't know him, he's no friend of mine."

Then a hand was shaking Mr. Saeed awake.

"Wake up, Isa," said Mrs. Saeed.

"Mr. Saeed opened his eyes.

"I want you to see something." Mrs. Saeed was looking down at Mr. Saeed with a strange expression on her face.

Mr. Saeed dragged himself out of bed and went downstairs. He followed his wife in a slow circle through the living room, into the dining room and finally into the kitchen. All three rooms had a trail of food running through them.

The living room had a few bowls of fruit on the floor. The dining room table had two heads of lettuce and a half a cucumber sitting on it beside an open jar of peanut butter and a pile of unopened tuna fish cans. There were cereal boxes on the table and a bowl with some cereal and milk in it. The open milk jug was in the center of the table. The kitchen counters were also loaded. There was everything from an opened bottle of corn oil to cucumber peelings and pitted prunes. The refrigerator door was wide open.

"What on earth happened?" asked Mrs. Saeed.

"Wow!" said Muhammad, who had just come downstairs. "That must have been some midnight snack!"

Mr. Saeed didn't know whether to laugh or to cry.

Jamaal and Fatima arrived on the scene.

"What happened?" asked Fatima.

"I didn't do it," said Jamaal.

Mrs. Saeed closed the refrigerator.

"Come on, everybody, come on out in the living room."

The whole family went into the living room and sat down.

"Abdul Jabbar is a little different," said Mr. Saeed, knowing that that was a big understatement. "What I mean is, he doesn't seem to be 'all there' upstairs."

"You mean he's 'cracked'," said Jamaal.

"It's called 'mentally challenged', Jamaal," said his older sister.

"Whatever you call it doesn't matter," continued Mr. Saeed. "The point is, he might need our help and for sure he'll need a lot of patience. He's our guest, and we should treat him with the same courtesy as we would treat any other guest, even if it takes more work. So, you children help your mother clean up the mess and I'll see if I can reach Uncle Anwar on the telephone."

When everyone got up, Mr. Saeed remained seated for a moment. He was thinking about how things were in Pakistan. They didn't have hospitals or fancy homes for the handicapped or mentally disturbed. Things were taken care of in a somehow more natural way. The people in a neighborhood or a town took care of each other. If there was someone with special needs, they were watched over by everyone else. If that person could work or do business, so be it. If they could care for a family, they married. If they couldn't take care of themselves, then not only their families, but the whole community watched out for them. They took part and were accepted in the whole community's life. There weren't a lot of facilities or therapies, but even so, Mr. Saeed felt that that natural system he had witnessed growing up in Pakistan was truly human and real. At the end of the day, Abdul Jabbar was just another guest, to be treated like any other guest, with maybe an extra helping of patience.

Mr. Saeed tried to call his brother, but the operator said that all the international lines to Pakistan were busy. She asked Mr. Saeed to try again later. Mr. Saeed tried again about an hour later, but the lines were still busy. He asked the operator to place the call for him and ring him back when she got through. Meanwhile, he waited for his guest to make an appearance.

Finally, at about noon, Abdul Jabbar came upstairs. He looked terribly angry.

"Why didn't you wake me for the prayer?" He demanded.

"I tried," said Mr. Saeed.

"If you didn't look so much like your younger brother, I might wonder just what was going on here!" Abdul Jabbar's eyes narrowed. "You certainly don't act like your younger brother!" He turned on his heel and stormed back downstairs.

Mrs. Saeed had gone out after breakfast. Mr. Saeed and the children stayed at home. Mr. Saeed sat in the living room thinking. Time passed. This might take a little more patience than he'd realized. After almost an hour, Mr. Saeed sent Jamaal downstairs to check on Abdul Jabbar. Time passed. After another fifteen minutes he sent Fatima down. Finally he sent Muhammad. Muhammad came back upstairs smiling.

"Paratha*!"

"What?" asked Mr. Saeed.

"He says he wants paratha for breakfast, paratha and eggs. He's really hungry and it's really late."

"I see," said Mr. Saeed, who had eaten a good many parathas in his life, but had never actually made any. "Well, I'm afraid he'll have to eat simple toast. Serving the guest is one thing, but my parathas would be more like punishment."

Fatima appeared at the top of the stairs.

"You should see how Abdul Jabbar combs his hair," she said. "He's got this special oil he uses. It takes a lot of work to get it all to stand up like that. Then it sort of hardens."

"Dad!" called Jamaal. "Dad, look at this!" He came running into the kitchen with a brick in his hand. "It's a real Pakistani brick!" he said. "Abdul Jabbar's got a ton of them! He said I could keep this one! I've got to find an American brick to trade for it."

Mr. Saeed smiled; international brick trading.

"There are some old bricks in the garage," said

---

* (Pa-Ra-Ta) A large, round, flat bread, fried in butter.

Muhammad.

"I want one too," said Fatima.

"Okay," said Mr. Saeed, "but be careful."

When the children went out, Abdul Jabbar appeared at the top of the stairs. "Fatima's right," thought Mr. Saeed. "It must take a lot of work to make his hair stick up like that."

"Good morning," said Mr. Saeed.

"Good morning," said Abdul Jabbar, "what a lovely day!"

"How many eggs would you like?" asked Mr. Saeed.

"Six!" said Abdul Jabbar. "I take six!"

Mr. Saeed got out a larger skillet and cracked the eggs into it. When they were done he served them up with four pieces of toast.

"What's this?" asked Abdul Jabbar.

"Eggs and toast," said Mr. Saeed.

Abdul Jabbar's eyes narrowed. "No paratha?" he said.

Mr. Saeed shrugged.

"Your brother always serves me paratha," said Abdul Jabbar.

"I don't think you'd like to eat my paratha," said Mr. Saeed.

Abdul Jabbar heaved a great sigh. He looked dejected. Then his face suddenly brightened. "Respected elder brother," he boomed. "What sights of America will you show me today, the Statue of Liberty?"

"Well, the Statue of Liberty is pretty far from here. Maybe you could see it on your way back to Pakistan."

"No, it will probably be late by that time. It's better we do it now."

"Well, I don't know," said Mr. Saeed. "At the moment, I'm waiting for a phone call from my brother. I'm sure we'll find some sights though."

One of Abdul Jabbar's eyebrows went up at the mention of Mr. Saeed's brother, but then he seemed to notice his eggs and devoted himself to the food. "By the way," he said through a mouthful of eggs. "Your shower overflows . . . I don't know, I tried clearing it out with lots and lots of water, even stamping on it, everything. It just overflows." When Abdul Jabbar looked up from his eggs, Mr. Saeed was gone. "Now, where did he go?" he thought.

Mr. Saeed was downstairs, on his hands and knees, trying to towel up the water that had spread out across the basement floor. "Three days," he kept repeating to himself, "only three days." He couldn't remember the last time he'd had his patience tested like this. "Well, it's good for me," he thought, "character building."

Mr. Saeed thought he heard the telephone ring. He leaned his ear toward the stairway. Nothing. "Was that the phone?" he called upstairs.

"What?" called back Abdul Jabbar, hanging up the telephone.

"Was that the phone?"

"Yes, I'm still alone!" Abdul Jabbar glanced happily at his empty plate. Still, there was something missing. Paratha. There was nothing like a paratha in the stomach to set you up for traveling. He stepped into the kitchen and opened the refrigerator.

By the time Mr. Saeed got upstairs, Abdul Jabbar had finished two more eggs. He was just pushing himself back from the table, leaning back in his chair. There was a large contented smile on Abdul Jabbar's face that changed to a questioning grin and then a look of alarm as the chair kept going back, and back, out of control. There was a heavy creaking sound. Suddenly the chair legs collapsed, dropping both Abdul Jabbar and the chair straight down.

"Yeow!"

Mr. Saeed leapt forward. He helped Abdul Jabbar up to a standing position.

"No harm done, no harm done!" Abdul Jabbar repeated, brushing himself off as if he were covered in dust.

"I'm sure it can be fixed," he said, rubbing the back of his head.

Mr. Saeed stared at his guest and then at the chair.

"You are a wonderful host!" declared Abdul Jabbar,

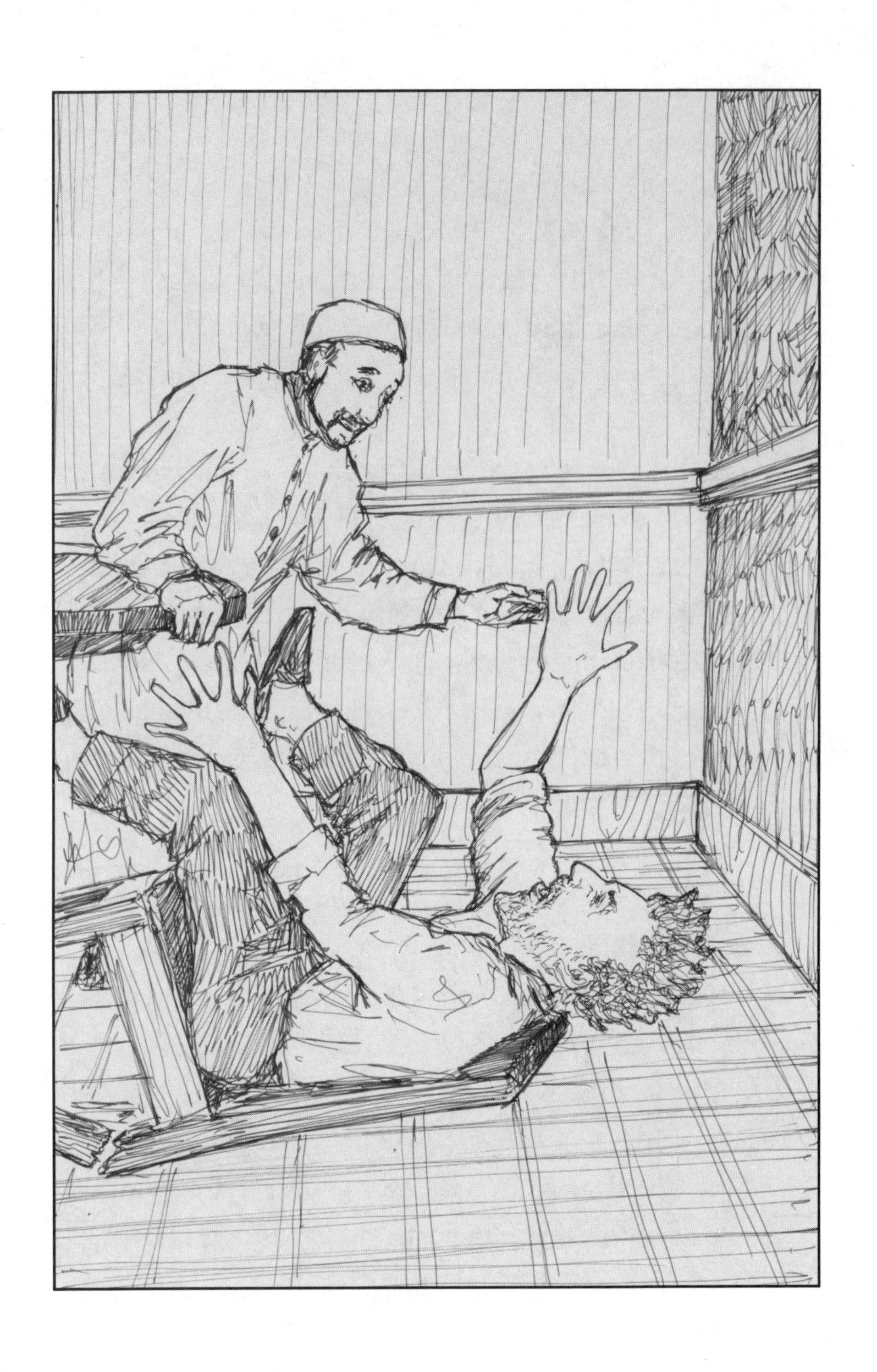

grabbing Mr. Saeed by the hand and shaking it wildly. “I shall remember you always!”

Just then there was a crash from the garage. Mr. Saeed ran to the door.

“We’re all right!” came Muhammad’s voice from the garage.

“What happened?” called Mr. Saeed, starting outside.

“The shelf dropped, but everyone’s all right.”

Mr. Saeed let out a sigh of relief.

“Uh . . . the car has a little dent in it . . .”

“What?”

“And the headlight . . .”

“What . . . ?” Mr. Saeed was entering the garage when the telephone rang. He glanced over at his children. They seemed to be all right. “Well, clean it up,” he said, and ran back into the house. Abdul Jabbar was nowhere in sight.

“Hello.”

“Is this Mr. Saeed?”

“Yes.”

“You were indisposed when I called you before; would you like me to connect you now?”

“I was what?”

“Indisposed,” said the operator.

Mr. Saeed tried to think.

“In-dis-posed,” said the operator. Do you want me to

connect you now?"

"Yes, operator . . . yes, I do." Mr. Saeed sighed and rubbed his forehead. Maybe now he'd make sense out of this whole thing.

"Assalaamu Alaykum!"

"Wa alaykum Assalaam. Anwar, this is Isa."

"Isa! How are you? Is everything all right?"

"Yes, everyone's fine. Anwar, I have a guest here from you."

"Oh?"

"Yes, did you send me a guest?"

"No," said Anwar. "I don't think so."

"His name is Abdul Jabbar. He says he's a friend of yours."

"I don't know any Abdul Jabbar," said Anwar.

"What?" Mr. Saeed paused for a moment. "Well, he certainly knows you! He says he's your boon companion!"

"My what?"

"Your boon companion!"

There was a long pause at the other end of the line as if Anwar were thinking. Suddenly there was a burst of high pitched, laughter. The laughter went on and on. Mr. Saeed found himself staring at the telephone.

"Anwar . . . Anwar . . ."

"Oh, oh, I'm sorry," said Anwar, pulling himself

together. “Did you say ‘boon companion’? And probably it’s getting pretty late over there too, isn’t it?”

“Yes,” said Mr. Saeed. “Yes, it is.” He didn’t understand a word of it.

The laughter continued on the other end of the line and then was cut short by a series of painful gasps.

“Oh . . . oh . . . What does he look like?”

Mr. Saeed described Abdul Jabbar and the laughter started again.

“Well, do you know him?” demanded Mr. Saeed.

“He’s the mailman,” gasped Anwar.

“He’s the what?”

“The mailman!” Anwar repeated. “He’s Abdul Jabbar, the mailman, the crazy one, you remember. The one with the bicycle with no tires on it, he’s got this thing about time, you remember!”

“La ilaha il Allah!” Suddenly it all became clear. Of course Mr. Saeed knew Abdul Jabbar. He could picture him now in his wrinkled kakhi uniform, wheeling his bicycle along. Of course Abdul Jabbar knew all about Anwar’s family and where they lived. Of course he knew their addresses!

His brother’s laughter started up again. “He disappeared from town about two weeks ago. It happens every year or two. But nobody knew where he’d gone this time.” There was more gasping over the phone. “So, how is he?”

"Oh, fine," said Mr. Saeed. "Fine . . ."

"How did he get over there?" asked Anwar.

"Good question," said Mr. Saeed.

"Well, his family will be happy to hear he's all right," said Anwar. "Be sure to give him my greetings."

"Right," said Mr. Saeed. He felt kind of in shock. The mailman?

"And call me back with the whole story!" shouted Anwar.

"I will," said Mr. Saeed, and he hung up the phone.

As Mr. Saeed descended the stairs, he wasn't at all sure of how to approach Abdul Jabbar about all of this. The decision was lifted from his hands. The basement was empty. The back door stood wide open and Abdul Jabbar's suitcase was gone. The guest room looked as if a hurricane had hit it. In the middle of the carpet there was a tiny clear space just big enough to hold a scribbled note. The note read, "Thank you so much, it's getting late. Your younger brother, Abdul Jabbar."

Mr. Saeed picked up the note and raced through the neighbors' back yards, calling Abdul Jabbar's name. Then he loaded the children in the car and drove around the neighborhood looking for him. He was so worried that he even called the police . . . But Mr. Saeed never saw Abdul Jabbar again. He did hear from him though. About six months later a very formal and flowery thank-you letter arrived in the mail from Pakistan. As Mr. Saeed read it, he wondered how many other letters had been received across the U. S. after the strange appearance and disappearance of the mystery "boon companion". Well, never mind, at least Abdul Jabbar was safe, that was the main thing.

The Saeeds had the thank-you letter framed and hung over the mantle piece where they also kept the "Pakistani brick". The whole family enjoyed them as reminders of their undisputed, champion, most favorite guest of all.

The Children's Stories Project

Director:
Dr. Omar Hasan Kasule

Coordinator:
Dr. Kadija Ahmed Ali

Advisory Panel:
Sharifa Alkhateeb
Nellie Jones Al-Saigh
Susan Douglass
Sarah Kasule
Kalid Tarapolsi